Make Your Child a Responsible Citizen

PRSE
of the Book

"A book of great inspiration, courage, and hope, every word rings with truth, kindness, and the beauty of the human spirit."

— Greenman Vijaypal Baghel
Renowned Environmentalist/Honored as Social Reformers of
India by Wikipedia

"What a beautiful, rich, and wise book on parenting. I wish I could give a copy to every new parent on the planet."

— Dinesh Verma
Author & CEO, Gullybaba Publishing House Pvt. Ltd.

"This book opens your mind, broaden your mind, and strengthen you as nothing else can."

— Dr. B.S. Sharma (MD, Ph.D.)
Author of "Yoga — Yoga & Ayurveda for all"

This book is selected by National Book Trust(NBT), Government of India at:

▶ Sharjah International Book Fair, 2016

MAKE YOUR CHILD

A RESPONSIBLE

CITIZEN

Learn how to Make your
Child Responsible effortlessly

Gullybaba Publishing House Pvt. Ltd.

GULLYBABA PUBLISHING HOUSE PVT. LTD.

ISO 9001 & ISO 14001 Certified Co.

Regd. Office: 2525/193, 1st Floor, Onkar Nagar-A, Tri Nagar, New Delhi-110035 (Near Kanhaiya Nagar Metro Station)

Branch Office: 1A/2A, 20, Hari Sadan, Ansari Road, Daryaganj, New Delhi-110002

Ph.: 9350849407, 011-27387998

E-mail: info@gullybaba.com

Websites: GullyBaba.com, GullybabaKids.com

Revised Edition: 2019

ISBN: 978-93-81970-63-8

To parents everywhere:
I wish you
Peace, patience, wonder and humor
For bringing up children to keep their joy, natural acceptance
of diversity, and capacity for wonder. May we instill in their hearts
the desire to see all people as their brothers and sisters, to develop
a consciousness of being part of one earth and one people, and
to promote justice, goodwill, and understanding.

Wishing you happy parenting.

Contents

- Take Stand for Your Self-respect
- Help Yourself
- When Chores Become Bigger Responsibilities
- Heroic Deeds
- Better to Have
- How Can I Be of Help to Someone?
- Cope with Courage
- Qualities of Being Resilient
- Qualities of Being Social
- Choice of Good Friends
- Respond to Your Feelings
- Sharing your Experiences

Few Words

As living creatures need air, food and water to survive on this planet, similarly human beings need a strong moral character to survive and succeed in the world of ethics besides requiring all these first three sources of survival. So when a child is born, his/her parents try to take best possible care of him/her that includes caring about his/her health, food, shelter, clothes and even toys for him/her. But when the child starts growing up, the parents become more concern about his/her character, which is one of the most important aspects of social life. A characterless individual is always looked down upon in the society with disgust and criticism. So character of an individual is the first and foremost thing to decide how good or bad a man is.

As witnessed widely that a full grown up or old parrot cannot learn to repeat or recite what you tell it, similarly it is extremely upheaval task to teach character-building to an adult. Therefore, there is need to groom one's child to become a good gentleman right from his childhood. In this pursuit, the parents need to teach and guide the child properly, thereby teaching him the lessons required to build a strong moral character. Keeping all these crucial aspects in view, I have put my humble but consistent efforts to bring out this book, especially for those parents and children who are desirous of learning character-building and want their children mark their presence in the society. The process and methods taught in this book are effectively constructive that are explained lucidly to easy understanding of children and even their parents as well. The book comprising 6 chapters suffices in teaching the relevant things required in building a strong moral character and developing a child into an ideal human being. I hope it will serve the purpose.

– Dinesh Verma

Acknowledgements

I acknowledge the almighty GOD or universal energy which has brought precious words of wisdom in front of my eyes, the wisdom to touch the soul of those words and creativity to present some of them to parent in YOU.

Out of the large repository of words few words I would like to acknowledge:

When I first helped my newborn son, I looked at him with tenderness and wondered and thought to myself, you are the most precious gift from God. I don't own you. I am here to help you find your way, to love you, and to let you go.

Susie Risho, Mother of Three Grown Boys

And I am a practising parent trying to touch the soul of above words.

I would like to put in my appreciation and acknowledgement for my family members, relatives, friends and Team of Gullybaba Publishing House Pvt. Ltd. and GullybabaKids.com.

I convey my special thanks to all the kids with whom we experimented and played activities and all those who entertained and taught me.

No work can find success without the most important part, that is, YOU, The READERS. I wholeheartedly thank all those who took pain in the making of the book.

-Dinesh Verma

Introduction

"Parenthood remains the greatest single preserve of the amateur."
~*Alvin Toffler*

As home is the first school for children, parents are the first teachers for them. When a child takes birth he depends upon his parents for each and every thing that he needs. And then, he understands only the language of his parents, especially the mother's. He learns to wear clothes, tie his shoe lace, put his tie, and he also learns to read and write from his parents. Lifestyle of parents is a source of auto-learning for their children. Thus, a home is the place where growing and grooming of children go hand-in-hand.

Among all kinds of learning, understanding the values of good character and how to develop such virtue merit vital importance in human life. Therefore, this book has been written with an aim of inculcating such virtues in children as can benefit them throughout their life. At the same time, parents are also guided how to make their children an ideal human being with a strong character. If a child has a strong moral character with a passion to serve his fellow beings, his country and humanity in general, he will be regarded as an asset not only to his family, school or his country, but also for the entire humankind.

This book will always be a perfect guiding light to the children as well as their parents. Besides, each chapter has been explained in such a way as can neither let the children, nor their parents get bore and lose their interest while reading this book.

✗ ✗ ✗

History will judge us by the difference we make in the everyday lives of children.

-Nelson Mandela

What Is a
Good Moral Character?

"You have to support your children to have a healthy relationship."
~ *Connie Sellecca*

I t is rightly said, "When wealth is lost, nothing is lost; when health is lost, something is lost; when character is lost, everything is lost." So, character merits paramount importance in our life. If you want to make your character strong, you have to adopt certain qualities, temperament or values that give a perfect turn to our way of thinking, actions and reactions, and also develop good feelings. So a good or strong character consists of the following virtues:

- Empathy or Compassion
- Honesty and Fairness
- Self-discipline

- Justness in Judgement

- Respect for Elders

- Self-respect

- Courage

- Responsibility

- Altruism

- Patriotism

Empathy or Compassion

Empathy or compassion means understanding others' condition and needs and feeling them in a way as if it is happening to you. It makes you to come forward to help those who are in crisis or pain. Empathy also makes us feel the happiness and enthusiasm of others rather than having annoyance and desperation on others' victories and successes.

The sense of empathy or compassion can be promoted by teaching our children the virtue of others' concern and feelings. For example, suppose that your child has beaten one of his classmates. The victim is weaker than your child. At that time, it is your responsibility as a parent to inculcate in your child the feeling of compassion telling him to think how painful has been your beating to your classmate. And if your child starts thinking in a way that he also might have felt the same degree of pain if he was beaten by someone else, at that time he will have the virtue of empathy in him. And thus, he will develop the first quality of strong character.

What Parents can do?

If you, as a parent, show compassion for others who are in need and help the victims of poverty, disease or accident in the presence of your child, he will watch you how you perform this good act. Moreover, it becomes your duty to explain and encourage your child to follow your footsteps in such philanthropic acts that will help him develop the sense of compassion and empathy.

Whenever you happen to pass along with your child through a beggar who really deserves alms, you must help him and urge your child to always take such initiative to help the needy people. This act will make your child cherish the virtue of empathy in him.

Being Honest and Fair

Honesty of a person lies in avoiding the act of misleading someone for one's own benefit. Honesty can also be exemplified in such a way as if someone finds thousands of rupees and valuables fallen on the road. If he wanted, he could have stashed away these valuables for his personal use. But he does not do so. Instead, he goes to police station and deposits these valuables there so that the person who has lost these valuables may collect from there. Thus, by doing this act, he gives a good example of honesty.

Fairness pertains to acting in a just way and making any decision on the basis of available evidence, not on partiality or prejudice. For example, if someone is in the position of selecting the applicants to any post in an organisation of company. Among the candidates if someone is found to be among his relatives, close friends or from his native place. But he selects only those candidates who deserve for the posts by virtue of their eligibility conditions, qualification and ability, and does not select those who are not able even they happen to be very near and dear to him. By doing so, he gives the best example of fairness in dealing.

What Can Parents Do?

- If you have watched any movie in which honesty is depicted by any character of the film, you must get your child watch at least that particular scene of the movie. It will not only excite your child to adopt the policy of honesty but he will also try to implement such act in his life.

- You can tell your child the moral stories in which honesty and fairness are promoted by its character. You can also apprise him with such events that you might have gone through in your life and that pertains to honesty and fairness. After all, you always keep your child urging him not get swayed by any glittering and attractive things that force him to adopt dishonest way. Keep asking him to be adhered to the virtue of honesty.

- You can explain fairness to your child by some performing practical act that will exert more influence upon him/her. For example, if there are three children, including your own son or daughter. Just take 6 toffees from a shop and distribute two toffees to each child. Since all the three children get two toffees each from you and you do not show any partiality in giving your child more toffees or others less, this is called a fair distribution.

✓ Dad, why are you taking my elder brother to have dinner in our neighbour's marriage ceremony, not me?
✓ Yes, because in the last marriage ceremony only two persons were invited from our family. And then I considered you to enjoy the feast along with me. So, it will not be fair if I again take you to have feast instead of your elder brother, because this time also only two invitees are there from our family.
✓ I've understood Dad; it's your honest and fair decision. You have given a good example of honesty and fairness by doing this.

Self- discipline

Self-discipline can be defined in various ways, self-discipline is the ability to control yourself from doing something that is not good for your health, for someone else or even anyone in any manner. If you adopt self-discipline in your life, you ascertain a set of realistic goal and strictly follow some Do's and Don'ts. If you are swayed away by the charm of any enjoyable act that is bad for you or humanity then automatically you lose the virtue of self-discipline.

Self-discipline always needs from you the persistence and adherence to long-term obligations, i.e. ignoring instant pleasure for later fulfilment. It also includes never allowing your emotions, such as anger, envy and greed etc. to dominate over your patience and perseverance.

If children learn self-discipline, it helps them regulate their activities and provides them the willpower to take right decisions at right time and make best choices. On the contrary, failure to adopt self-discipline leads the children to developing such behaviour and activities that ultimately spoil their career and even life also. Therefore, self-discipline plays a very important role, especially in children's life.

What Can Parents Do?

- Teach your child the virtue of self-discipline. Try to let your child understand self-discipline by your practical examples. If your child or any child in your family or acquaintance is a junk-food addict. Simply, tell him the harms of such food and the way he should abstain from it. It may inculcate in him the power to control himself from indulging in junk-food.

- It generally happens in most of the families where the children are found to be in the habit of sleeping late in night. They do so because they watch television, play games on mobile or simply chat online with their friends. In such case, help your child develop a sense of punctuality and competence. You can make your child aware of the disadvantages of sleeping late and doing all such things. Simultaneously, teach him/her to have control over his/her desire and following the healthy routines with discipline.

- You can show your child the parade done by soldiers either live or on television etc. There remain a number of soldiers in one flight (group). When they move in parade, they start moving and stop instantly and simultaneously on hearing the command of their commander or flight senior.

This is a perfect example of self-discipline where soldiers do all the movements in parade by having full control over themselves.

Justness In Judgement

Doing just and right judgement always saves man from losses and sufferings. A child of strong moral character can judge well as he has the ability of thinking over right and wrong, and all that pertains to taking judgement or decision.

It can be taught to children by creating such scenario as often happens with them. For example, your summer vacation is going on in a hot summer of May and June. The temperature is touching 40 degree Celsius, and you want to play cricket in the scorching sun! It's not a just or right judgement. If you consider to play in the evening when the heat subsides, it will be just or good judgement.

What Can Parents Do?

- Teach your child to think over from all points-of-view before taking any decision. You can exemplify by telling a story of a student like thus: there was a student who was interested in language and literature. He used to score rich marks in such subjects. But after doing his S.S.C, his parents ordered his son to take commerce. Under his parent's pressure, he took commerce but did not do well, which was not a good judgement, nor was it just. Had the parents given the student liberty to go for language and literature, the child could have excelled in that stream.

- Create a situation asking your child to choose one from the two given options. Just offer your child asking whether he would like to have a television set with Dish connection at his drawing room or a computer/laptop with Internet connection. After knowing his decision, just ask him the reason of choosing that option. On hearing the reasons, you can understand how better his judgment was. At the same time, you can also explain him the reason behind choosing one particular option. If the child chooses computer with Internet connection, it would be a better judgement, because it's a multi-purpose machine, whereas on television you can watch different programmes, games or movies only.

- More often than not, let your child take his own decision while facing any challenge in life. Of course, you can guide him if he is found to be on the wrong track or taking irrational judgement. Simultaneously, tell him the reason why you have guided him.

✓ Aslam! Do you know, my friends Jack and Janardhan were insisting me to accompany them on a week-long tour to Manali?

✓ I was fascinated by his offer but I know I've got my exams just after a couple of weeks. So if I moved on an excursion tour at such a crucial juncture, I will lose my studies and I may do bad in the exams.

✓ You've taken absolutely just and right judgement at this moment that proves your ability to judge well.

Respect for Elders

If you respect others, especially your elders, you are respecting yourself. By giving respect to your elders, your value in their eyes is enhanced automatically. Respect can be shown in various manners. One can talk and act in a civilised manner avoiding insult, unkind remarks and abstaining from slang and rough language.

You can earn respect by being courteous and considerate of others and taking care of the rights, beliefs and well-being of others in your neighbourhood. It will be highly appreciable if you treat others fairly irrespective of their caste, creed, race, sex, age, religion or ethnicity.

According to a research, children learn to respect others only after they are treated with respect by their elders. More punitive action taken with harsh treatment of hard criticism and beating often instil negative and rebelling attitude among them. So an ambience of respect and good manner must be created and maintained not only at school and home, but also at other places where children are chanced to meet and interact with others.

What Can Parents Do?

- Every good and bad manner starts from home. So it's incumbent upon the parents to focus on the necessity of good manner and mutual respect being practised at their home. The parents are responsible to address their child with respect so that the child may learn such virtues of giving and earning respect right from his childhood.

- Anger and enmity are arch enemies of respect and etiquette. It is often seen that people start abusing and using derogatory language in anger. The parents can teach their children not to used abusive language in such condition; of course they express their anger by telling the fact in front of the person who is the reason behind the anger but it should also be express in a civilised manner, i.e. the best example of giving respect

- Even if you are not receiving a call from any professional or the persons whom you respect more, just act in a way as if you are talking to someone on phone in the presence of your child. While talking on phone, use as much words of respect as you can. It will give a good impression upon your child and he/she will think that this is the way of talking to someone. Thus, he/she will always follow such a nice and respectable of conversation.

✓ Raju, yesterday an interesting thing happened with me.
✓ After landing at Sahar Airport, I took a taxi for Andheri East. While talking to the taxi driver, I addressed him 'Sir'.
✓ The driver was so influenced by such addressing that he was overwhelmed with respect and while getting down at Andheri, he not only helped me unload my luggage but also said good-bye with folded hands.
✓ And then, I understood that giving respect to others always pays you more.

Self-respect

Self-respect does not mean ignoring others' respect or having ego in any manner. Self-respect pertains to having satisfaction in an appropriate behaviour and accomplishments made by strenuous efforts. Such person would never discourage others from adopting such virtue; rather he would encourage others to move on righteous path and always avoid bragging or boasting of his abilities or achievements.

Self-respect does not mean over-estimation of oneself. A person of self-respect never gets awed by others' wealth or resources. He never yields to others in the time of difficulty nor does he lose the virtue of patience and perseverance. Encouragement, especially to children, is a cardinal essence of strengthening the value of self-respect.

However, it doesn't mean that children should be encouraged to adopt anything that ultimately may prove to be a factor behind spoiling their character. From time to time, they should also be criticised honestly for their acts and work because criticism always works as antibiotics for them. One thing should always be kept in mind that is: Do not bring children's personality under criticism; you may criticise their activities and way of doing anything so that they may mend their ways and perform well in much better way.

What Can Parents Do?

- Always encourage your child to establish a positive identity that concentrates on his truth and talent.

- Lay emphasis on the fact that character is built on right and timely judgements and actions a person takes in his daily life.

- Give company to your child, helping him have access to his full potential by inspiring him to cherish talents, set accessible goals and regard himself as a man of worth and perfection.

- Teach your child the way of choosing good values. Help him think rationally and act properly as to what are worthy goals and what are the exact means of reaching those goals.

- Teach your child that if he/she wishes or greets an elder even that elder may be illiterate, poor and in shabby condition; he (the child) simply enhances his self-respect by giving respect to that elder person and simultaneously, the child's respect in the eyes of that person increases.

✓ Harry, why are you so sad today?
✓ Uncle, I could not score the desired marks while I had worked hard to prepare for the exams. My self-respect is hurt badly.
✓ You need not worry at all about what others are saying on your poor marks. Instead, resume your studies with more diligence for your next exam. Failure or scoring poor marks is a part of life that teaches man as to where he has made the mistake and how it will be mended.
✓ Don't lose your heart. Maintain your self-respect, devote yourself to your studies; the day will come that you will excel in your exams and thus, every criticizing mouth will be shut automatically.

Courage

Courage can be defined in various ways. Courage is the ability to overwhelm your fear in the way of reaching your desired goal. Courage also means facing the challenges bothering least about the physical dangers that may cause to you, but still you continue to remain steadfast and move with confidence to confront with the challenges and meet your purpose. Having courage does not mean being reckless, thoughtless and inattentive in taking any initiative where unnecessary risks and dangers are involved.

Resilience (the ability to spring back into shape or earlier position) is also an indication of courage. Suppose you happen to wrestle with a boy much stronger than you. He pushes you to the ground by his physical strength causing injury to you, and yet you stand up and resume fighting with him; this is called resilience and a perfect example of courage.

What Can Parents Do?

- Train your child to be brave in all the conditions. Admire him for an act of bravery and never make mockery of his work where courage is involved.

- Teach your child that taking caution and thinking before taking any initiative do not mean losing courage. Tell him/her that showing courage without precaution is idiocy that may invite dangers and even failure to him/her.

- Advise your child to beware of such friends who boast him of doing such acts that bring nothing but endanger his life or may cause injury to him.

- Emphasise your child on maintaining calm and composure, particularly in panicky conditions; this is an example of showing courage that may always lead him to safety and success.

- Teach your child never breach the law, rules and regulations while showing courage in any act of performance. Before using courage, just think over the matter whether it will be a breach of law. If it is so, there is no need to show courage.

✓ Dad, some of the children were making unnecessary noise in our school library while the librarian had gone for a tea-break.
✓ Then what did you do?
✓ I told them to maintain silence as others were getting disturbed by their noise, but they reacted harshly threatening me of dire consequences. However, I complained this to the Librarian and the Principal also.
✓ But what about the threatening they have given to you?
✓ They haven't done anything being afraid of expelled from the school and being scared of punished by their parents also.
✓ You have shown your courage, you have proved yourself a brave boy. Well done! I am proud of you.

Responsibility

Responsibility means honouring your given words, promises, commitments and doing justice to self-assigned tasks and also other tasks you take up to accomplish. Responsibility also means accepting the consequences of anything you have done.

A responsible person never makes excuses for his actions or doesn't resort to blaming others for anything gone wrong.

Children must be taught the virtue of responsibility right from their childhood. If they are taught this, they will make themselves strong enough to overcome the difficulties in life. They will depend less upon others and enable themselves to face most of the challenges of life without yielding to others.

What Can Parents Do?

- When you promise to give anything to your child, fulfil it. And when you fulfil the promise, at the same time you remind him/her that you have fulfilled your responsibility, which is a better example of being responsible.

- Teach your child not to bother about the pain and difficulty experienced in fulfilling the responsibility. At the same time, appreciate the honour and affection he/she gets by being an epitome of responsibility.

- Inspire your child to explore more about the world and all in it and how his/her actions may influence the world.

✓ Mom, I'm going to play cricket.
✓ Rahul, it's not even 5 o'clock, and you are going to playground! Do you remember you have been assigned the duty of serving medicine to your ailing grand-dad?
✓ Oh mom, I'm so sorry. I was so excited to play that I forgot all about it.
✓ Now this is the medicine in my hand which I am going to give to my beloved grand-dad.
✓ Yes, this is called responsibility and being a responsible person.

Altruism

Altruism means the principle/practice of unselfish concern for others or devotion to others' welfare even to the cost of yourself. The virtue of altruism naturally comes out of the empathy and compassion an individual has for others. In other words, altruism means sacrificing your own comfort for the sake of others who deserve more than you. It generally happens in public place such as waiting lounge, park, bus, train, tram, hospital, religious shrines and so on.

Suppose you are travelling while sitting comfortably in a crowded bus or metro train where all seats including those reserved for ladies, senior citizens and physically challenged are occupied. And then an old man gets on the bus. You instantly leave your seat for that old man so that he should not bear the brunt of crowd. It is one of the best examples of altruism.

What Can Parents Do?

- Teach your child the virtue and values of practising altruism in life.

- Tell your child how to create, grab and utilise the opportunity of serving the deserving persons in various ways that will simply exemplify what exactly altruism means.

- Persuade your child to adopt the practice of altruism, although facing a bit of pain and difficulty is but natural in this way. However, one should not bother about such difficulty or pain as taking pain for others enhances his honour in the eyes of those who are benefited from him.

- Convince your child to relish pleasure in bringing pleasures to others who need more than you. Thus, the pain of practising altruism turns one's pain into pleasure. Also teach your child the fact that if everybody starts practising altruism, this world will turn into model of paradise.

✓ On reaching my home in Kolkata, I asked my mom to let me sleep soon as I could not sleep well in the train.
✓ Why couldn't you sleep?
✓ Most of the eastbound trains leaving from Delhi remain packed. Even reservation compartments also remain crowded. When I was going to sleep on my reserved berth, an old woman accompanied by his son, boarded the train at Kanpur. They could not get their berths reserved and tried to sleep on the floor. I gave my berth to the old ailing women to sleep, while I continued to sit on the end of the birth. Anyway, I am happy that I became able to help someone in need.
✓ I am proud of my son. God bless you; you have exemplified altruism in the best possible way.

Patriotism

A good citizen is always a good patriot. A patriot is always devoted to his country and countrymen in various manners. Doing anything good for one's nation and even thinking constructive about one's nation is a virtue of patriotism. Praising good aspects of one's country and claiming them across the world will also be categorised as a principle of patriotism. But if you are praising excessively any product, aptitude, military or government policy that is proved to be harmful to the citizens of the country or these are not as appreciable as they need to be then it will be chauvinism rather than patriotism.

Patriotism is the passion of love and loyalty cherished for one's country.

It is generally said, "Charity begins at home". This adage is symbolic to saying that the work of patriotism starts from one's locality and society. If you take part in cleaning, medication and welfare of your locality in any manner you can, it means you are serving your country and that will be a good example of patriotism.

If you are abroad (in a foreign country), your first preference in any sort of considerations should by your countrymen. There are some Indian businessmen in Dubai, London and New York who though employ the people from other countries also; their first preference remains to be Indians. By doing so, they help India's economy flourish. Thus, one can serve one's country by any manner, thereby exuding patriotism well by such acts.

What Can Parents Do?

- Take your child to art gallery, museums and historical places where story of patriotic people, their courage and sacrifices are inscribed on monuments. By seeing all such things, your child can cherish the sense of patriotism in his heart.

- Tell them the story of freedom fighters of our country by whose sacrifice we are enjoying the freedom of our country. It will make your child realise how devoted they were to their country.

- Teach your child that besides joining the defence forces like Army, Navy and Air Force, he can also serve and glorify the name of his country by inventing, innovating and bringing something new to his country.

- Acquaint your child with the fact that our soldiers spend the toughest life at the borders and bordering areas. Their agile and active presence at the borders allows us to sleep well in nights and earn our livelihood during day without worrying about outside invasions. So paying respect to soldiers is also a sign of patriotism.

✓ Kamal, it's time to come into action and clean garbage and other littered things from our locality as the cleaning staff of our municipality have gone on indefinite strike.

✓ Yes, you are right. Let's call other boys from each house of our locality as the condition has gone from bad to worse.

✓ Thanks God! Almost all the boys turned up on last Sunday with brooms in their hands and a hired matador was used to dispose the garbage. It was a clarion call which everybody listened to and swung into action to give an ideal example of being the good citizens and patriots of India.

✗ ✗ ✗

Having a baby is a life-changer. It gives you a whole other perspective on why you wake up every day.

~Taylor Hanson

How Can We Teach Our Children Character-building?

"I do think that there's an art form to parenting, and I have nothing but admiration for those who do it well."
~ *Elizabeth Berg*

The old and meaningful saying is, "Action speaks louder than voice". It's just to tell your child and forget about it. But the values of this constructive saying lie in your actions. Children mostly follow that which their parents do. Thus, they learn about building strong moral character when their parents and other elders in their family perform such actions that remain packed with character-building essences.

Therefore, the parents can set the following goals to let their children learn character-building:

- Behave in the presence of your child in a way that sets a good example of a high moral character.

- Communicate with your child maintaining a high level of standard and create such a situation that allows your child to expect more learning from you.

- Guide your child on how to be responsible and caring. Guidance also involves keeping a watch on your children.

- Besides all these constructive sources, you need to make use of good literature that will help your children learn and build a strong moral character.

Making Actions a Source of Learning

Most of the times, we teach our children the mannerism, social etiquette and other virtues verbally where no action is involved. It is also a good thing, but they learn anything more from our action and behaviour. Since home is the first school of the children, their grooming in learning to build a strong character also starts from here.

When we talk to our wives, gossip with our friends, deal with our clients/customers, interact with our neighbours, converse with our elders and treat our guests, behave with our servants and outsiders like beggars, taxi/auto drivers and so on; all these are watched by our children who later try to replicate them.

In fact, children inherit everything from their ancestors, especially from their parents—be it good things or bad. As a father if you abuse your wife or servant, your child will also use abusive language for them. Your children are just like parrots in action. If you keep smiling, your child even from the phase of infancy will keep smiling like you. If you scold others in your family members, your child will assume it a way of talking and thus, he will simply follow your scolding habit.

Therefore, the need of the hour is that first you behave well; your child will behave well automatically. If something goes wrong in the presence of your child and you get angry over this happening, don't abuse and raise the volume of your rebuking voice over someone; try to have control over your anger and maintain composure. It's the time of your test how you deal with the oddities. By maintaining composure, show yourself that such wrong or harmful happenings are a part of life and one should not get angry or panicky over these things because that is not the solution to the problems. Believe it by watching this wise action, your child will also learn to tackle embarrassing things with ease, and that will help him build a strong moral character.

Apart from behaviour and etiquette, you can also take such actions that practically elucidate the difference between wants and needs. Besides being fascinated by the items used by elders in home, children get attracted to the dresses, watches and other items used by his/her classmates belonging to rich families. For this, you have to adopt austerity (living satisfactorily without unnecessary comforts or things) up to a certain extent. When your child sees you high branded watch on your wrist, he will also insist on having such a watch. But if you put on a simple watch of average cost, he will not dare to ask for costly watch. You can also convince him saying that all the watches give the same time, when then to wear costly watch!

Thus, your child's insistence on demanding costly or high branded watch is an example of wants, whereas putting on a simple watch of an average price is a need. Thus, practice of austerity also helps your child build a strong moral character and that must be followed by children.

✓ Dad, why are you putting all your used shaving blades into a small tin box?

✓ I'm putting it into this box for the safety of the stray cows, bulls and goats which are often found searching for edibles in the accumulated garbage and eating them hastily. If I throw these blades openly into the garbage, they may eat them along with other things. Thus, these blades may cause severe injury to their mouths; and if not, inside their stomachs.

✓ Oh Dad, how kind and caring you are!

✓ It's a sign of having a strong character and being a caring citizen.

Communicate with Your Child

Communication gap always makes the progress of any positive thing slow or ends it before reaching its accomplishment. So what parents need to do is, keep communicating with their children raising the issue of character-building and suggesting the ways to build a strong moral character. Simultaneously, while communicating with your children, you also need to set a high standard of everything that you go through in your day-to-day life. Setting high standard will always keep your children's moral character high and appreciable.

While at home, parents are strongly advised to give quality time to their children. Here, giving quality times means to communicate with your children by initiating constructive talk. What is this constructive talk? The constructive talk is meant for constructing a strong character of your children. While interacting with your children, you need to focus on the essence of a good character.

First of all, you are supposed to acquaint your children with the virtue and principles of being a man of strong character. You have to explain them as to what benefits can be enjoyed by building a strong character and what problems one has to face on being devoid of such character. Thereafter, you need to guide them how to build such an appreciable character. You also have to apprise them that while adopting good things to build a strong character, they will confront with lots of oddities and ordeal. They will have to go through a litmus test to prove themselves the persons of strong moral character. All these are possible if you sit together with your children in a pleasant ambience and communicate with them inculcating the virtues of a good moral character.

- ✓ Dad, today our sitting together and communicating with each other merit vital importance in our life.
- ✓ Tell me what you have learned by our communication and setting the standard of our words and action.
- ✓ Having communication with each other and raising such relevant topics as help us build a strong character are of sterling worth. The standard of our thinking and studying something has been raised, which will prevent us from falling into low standard of conversation and action.
- ✓ That's good. I also attain pleasure in teaching you such valuable things that will never let you down anywhere in the world.

Guidance

Guidance comprises not only coaching your children to righteous way of life but it also involves keeping a watch on your children, lest they may swerve from the right track. As parents, your actions, your words, and your communication help your child learn how to build a strong character; and guidance is also a kind of teaching or coaching. However, there is a slight difference in it.

If you do not guide your child, he may go to other guides or coaches to learn the values of life; and it is not guaranteed whether he will get the right guidance from other coaches. As a father or mother, you are the best coach for your child because your child is attached to you emotionally, not professionally. So after guiding your child to the righteous path of life and inculcating the virtue of strong character in him, just have a watch whether he is implementing what you have taught so far. If you find him not implementing your given lessons or ignoring them deliberately, you keep reminding them sometimes politely and sometimes strictly as well, depending upon how your child responds to you.

✓ Vimlesh, let's hide those boys' clothes as they have gone to take bath in the pond. No, my father will punish me.

✓ How can your father come to know about it? Common, we will enjoy a lot when they come and get baffled to find their clothes missing.

✓ Yeah, come and hide their clothes here under this rock. O my God! My Dad is passing from here and he might have seen us hiding them. What will happen now?

✓ Yes boys, I have seen you trying to hide something under the rock. For your kind information. I am sure you have simply ignored what morality I have taught to you. This evidences that your character is weakening. Mind it! I'll not tolerate the repetition of such act from you.

✓ I'm so sorry Dad. I was misled by my friend. I promise you, any of such acts will not be repeated by me.

Good Literature

Good literature plays a paramount role in evolving a child into a man of strong character. Children often evince interest in listening to stories, and there is no dearth of didactic story books in the market that become an effective tool to teach them the character-building. There was a time when children's grandmother used to tell stories at bed-time and the kids would sleep, thereby learning many things from her. But today the scenario has changed. Apart from books in print form, they also have direct access to Internet where they find various moral stories and even the films made on them.

So it is strongly advisable to the children that they must select some books of moral stories. They may purchase or tell their parents to buy from the market, or they may download from the Internet. Parents and family elders encourage their children to read moral stories which are full of lessons. Study of such books will help them learn character-building. It's gradual process as they will develop the values of strong character and worth of being a good citizen.

- ✓ Sameer, do you know what a nice gift I've got from my uncle on my last birth day?
- ✓ What's that Sahil? Is it smart phone or swanky wrist watch?
- ✓ I knew you would say so. It's a book of moral stories. I have gone through a few stories and come to know how much virtues and character-building essences I was lacking in my life. It has become a powerful teaching tool that guides me to become a person of strong moral character.
- ✓ Oh, I was wrong Sahil. I used to prefer fascinating electronic items to books. But today I have also realised how valuable the books are in our life.

Start Question-Answer Session

After your child has read a story book, sit together with him/her and start a question-answer session on what he/she has read in the story. It is a result-oriented device of measuring what and how much your child has learned after going through the relevant literature. So just prepare a few pertinent questions to ask him/her. Children must know that the roles given to each individual to play in the story is called a character or actor.

Motivational Questions

- How did the characters (role played by the individual actor) in the story act?

- What were their motives?

- Who was the protagonist (hero)

- Who among the characters/actors played positive role (doing good things), and what was his/their motives?

- Who among the character/actors played negative role (doing bad or evil things), and what was his/ their motives?

Judgemental Questions

- Had the characters/actors in the story taken good decisions? Express your opinion.

Action-related Questions

- How did the characters/actors implement their decisions? What initiatives did they take in this regard? Did they face any impediment? If yes, how did they tackle the impediments?

Compassion-related Questions

- Were the characters/actors concerned about others' wellbeing?

- Was the end of the story good or bad? In whose favour was it good and in whose favour was it bad?

- How would the story have become favourable to all the characters/actors?

A Good Collection of Books

As said earlier, there is no shortage of books in the market or library. What matters the most is your choice of books. Of course, it will take time to decide which book will be the conducive for character-building. You need not worry about it as there is a good collection of books in the market as well as libraries. You may choose the ones like fiction and non-fiction books; the books of poetry, folk tales, fables and plays etc. Besides, there are also wonderful modern stories apart from timeless classics.

Need to be Careful

While choosing the book for character development, there is a need to be a bit careful whether the moral theme of story, non fictional literature, ply or poetry may be comprehensive to your child as all children are not always of similar choice. So keep discussing with your child as to which types of books he/she likes to read. With adequate patience, try to listen attentively to what ideas your child has in his/her mind. If his/her ideas are above the level of what you think for him/her, talk with him/ her with the same standard lest you should misunderstand him/her. Whatever books are chosen just read the parts of the story with your child and discuss on the moral of the story.

- ✓ Bunty, one thing I've learned from the Lion and Hare story.
- ✓ What have you learned Jaunty?
- ✓ Ego and idiocy always lead to destruction. Had the lion been wise to realise his reflection in the water and not shown his ego, he would not have jumped into the well to fight another lion which was actually his reflection. And thus, the hare used his wisdom to save not only his life but also those of other animals of the jungle.
- ✓ It consolidates the fact that though lion was physically powerful, lacked wisdom and the strength of character.

✗ ✗ ✗

"The voice of parents is the voice of gods, for to their children they are heaven's lieutenants." ~William Shakespeare

Creativities Through Activities

M ost of the parents set a routine of daily life, slashing time from their daily schedule to play with their children, go for a walk with them or at least initiate a constructive talk with them. But apart from their occupational activities, a major portion of parents' time is spent on gauging how much their children have learned from the books. This is also a good concern; but together with this, parents are also supposed to devote their time to their children doing such activities that result in creativities.

Childhood is a period when you, as parents, can mould your children to any desired shape and design; and that is possible with little efforts and devotion only. Teach your children that having a strong moral character doesn't mean to suppress one's emotion of expressing happiness and sadness. These are basic instincts and natural things. One should release one's joys by laughing and one's grief by crying.

If you do not become happy and do not express your pleasure of winning a game/sport and inversely, do not become sad on losing the game, the game will not have any meaning or value in life. But one thing always be kept in mind that is one may become sad for a while, but it doesn't mean to lose hope for good. Similarly, any activity that is adopted and continued must be creative. Here, to be creative means not only to create anything in solid form, but to develop such thing that helps the child strengthen his/her character, ability to think and power to prevail over any challenge in life.

As parents, if you give your quality time playing with your children, they will not only enjoy the play/sport but will also learn the how to apply to apply the wisdom and how to maintain perseverance and patience if there arises the need to do so. A physical activity involves the entire body as well as the brain that keeps the body strong and makes the individual mentally alert.

Learn from Others

There is a vast variety of people around and beyond you. Some of them are living with you and are very near to you in your family, school, relatives and friends, in your neighbourhood and so on, while there are also many people whom you know but they live away or far from you. However, every individual has some unique quality that may be good or bad also. Now it depends upon you what you extract from them in the form of learning from their activities and thoughts.

First of all, just observe the activities of the people who may be from different walks of life. They may be professionals, officers, teachers, businessmen, labourers and even the beggars. Just adopt all good things what you find exuded from their activities and reject what they misuse or cause harm to anyone in any manner.

What Can Parents Do?

- Let your child know that you are interested in learning new things from other people you meet or interact. Your actions comprising meeting people and interacting with them should let your child know how caring you are about your family. Together with this, you may also acknowledge your child about your hobbies and jobs. All these will increase the desired knowledge of your child and thus, he will develop in himself good activities which you may have taught him by your actions. Your amicable treatment to your neighbours, relatives and friends will always encourage your child to behave in the same ethical manner that gradually help him develop a strong character.

• As parents, you should develop the habit of reading some good books, magazines and periodicals etc. For this take your child to different libraries, bookstalls, and must visit a book fair if held in your town/city. Choose some good books and magazines and tell your child the benefits of reading such reading materials. After going through such books and magazine, your child may ask you some questions to clarify something that he might have read. It will be a good chance for not only elucidating the things he has asked but you may also add something relevant to this to your answers that will be doubly beneficial for him.

✓ As parents, teach your child to be tolerant, polite and amicable with others while meeting and interacting with them.

✓ But sometimes it is not sure that others will also respond in the same manner. They may turn harsh and rude; sometimes even their behaviour may turn harmful also.

✓ In such case, tell your child not be so innocent and tolerant. Tell him to just leave talking to them and be strict in his stand.

Gifts of Your Own Hands

There is no lack of occasions in our daily life. Festivals, marriage ceremonies and birth day parties are a frequently common happening in our society. Whenever you children are invited to attend a birth day party or any of such celebration, try to present the gifts made by your own hands because your self-made gifts have more emotions and love than those of bought from the market. Such gifts will touch the heart of the recipient and your love and respect in his/her eyes will be enhanced that ultimately helps a lot in strengthening your moral character as well as that of the recipient.

What Can Parents Do?

• Whenever your child is invited to any birth day party or any celebration from your relatives, friends or neighbours, advise him/her to make gift by hands rather than buying the same from the market. Help your child making the gift item and buying the accessories required for it. If you don't know how to make it, just go to YouTube where you can have several demos to learn and replicate. If not so, there are also books in the market in which gift making is taught with pictures.

• Besides presenting home-made gifts, you may also encourage and teach your child to enhance the pleasure of the party by playing a skit, a play, or performing a dance and singing etc. Such acts will bring your child much closer to the hosts and thus, your child may become a good source of learning art, culture and ethics for others.

• In addition to presenting the home-made gifts to friends, relatives and neighbours, it will be highly appreciable if you encourage your child to present such gifts to those in your neighbourhood or relatives who are poor or less privileged. This type of kind act will not only bring smile to their face added with respect and affection, but your honour will also be enhanced in the society and above-all in the eyes of Almighty God.

✓ Children know it well that giving anything to your beloved one or a needy one merits more values than taking from someone.

✓ Though it is a good habit to continue this practice, here children are strongly advised to consider giving such gifts to those who have no access to them due to their poverty or lack of resource.

Always Stick to Truth

Getting benefit by cheating or manipulating is always based on telling lies. Though you can have a momentary joy by doing this, you will lose your trust in others' eyes. So before such act spoil your trust, respect and personality, better you stick to truth and never get sways by artificial glitters.

What Can Parents Do?

• Referring the fable of "Wolf came wolf came" will concretely work to make your child understand the harms of telling lies and benefits of telling the truth.

• If your child has been misled or cheated by someone, just ask how all it happened to him/her;

how he/she was fascinated by the cheater; how he/she is feeling after being misled. Ask him/her why he/she did so and whether he/she will like to repeat the same act in future. If not, then why not. Such questions will make your child's concept clear in regarding telling truth vis-à-vis telling lies.

- When you find your child telling a lie, express your displeasure over it and explain him/her the consequences of this bad habit. Before that, you ask him/her what made him/her to tell lie before you. If he/she did so to get anything done or get any demand fulfilled by you, it could have been done in other righteous way also by telling the truth.

- Parents are also advised to become a model of truth, honesty and other virtues for your children. Try to do all good and noble activities in front of your child and explain him/her the value of doing such acts. If your child is an adolescent i.e. in teens, it demands more care, patience, and agility from you to deal with your child with due care and are of persuasion.

✓ Parents are strongly suggested not tell lie or do an act of pretention before your child. It may result in unexpected harm to your child as well as you.
✓ Try to be a model of goodness and qualities in the eyes of your children.
✓ Always remain steadfast to your words and commitment, no matter you may face some difficulties in this way, but it will leave good impression to your children.

The Art of Telling the Truth

Euphemism is a figurative speech in English literature that is often used to tell something serious and bitter in a calm and sweet way. Suppose any of your friends sang a song on an occasion. But in fact, he could not sing well and thus, bored the audience. If that friend asks you how he has sung, and you straightaway tell the truth that you didn't like his way of singing, he will simply get hurt by your outright opinion, although that is true.

So you can use your wisdom and respond him in such way as: "Yeah, your song was okay; however, it could have been much better if you would have sung in low scale paying caution to your rhythm. Responding in this way will not only help your child find where he/she is lagging behind and needs mending, but he will also have pride of having a parent who tell truth and does not praise anybody blindly.

Continue Your Efforts

One thing you always keep in your mind, i.e. success comes from efforts and experience, and experience is gained from bad experience that is failure. So if you could not succeed in your efforts, you should not drop your attempts. Your failure teaches you how to resume your preparation this time. Keep trying that will ultimately make you successful in your endeavours. Your will power to try again and again will make strong enough not only your character and personality but it will also strengthen your inner-self to face any challenge in life.

What Can Parents Do?

- In this fast urban lifestyle where everybody is found busy and resultantly tiring in earning livelihood for their families, it is but natural for parents to lose the natural charm on his face after coming home from the day-long strenuous work, and heavy traffic snarl added with the attack of pollution. However, the parents are still advised not to forget giving a smile to their children soon after entering home. Though you may be extremely frazzled at that time, but your smile and affectionate treatment will encourage your child to be morally strong like you.

- Whenever you take up a task to accomplish together with your child, use a timer because you and your child can measure the time consumed in completion of that task. This will help him/her learn to measure how much hard work and talent are required to complete which types of task.

- Try to make your child know that pleasures come after pains i.e. hard work, as you go to play or watch TV after doing homework or other chores. You become physically strong after doing physical exercise.

✓ Children must know it well that their hard work never goes in vain. It will result well in the long run.
✓ So carry on your efforts to overcome any challenge in life—no matter whether you fail in your first attempt or excel throughout your career.

Be Steadfast in Taking Decision

More often, you are caught in a situation when you find yourself unable to decide what to do and what to not. Your dilly-dallying in making any decision in the way of your career-building or character-building will make you weak. So if you happen to face any problem and see a solution then simply think over it without taking much time and come out with a firm decision.

What Can Parents Do?

- While thinking over any issue/matter to decide, keep giving voice to your thinking so that your child should hear your words and learn how think over before taking any decision.

- Make it a regular phenomenon to think over any matter in family along with your child, exchange your views in between and then take decision. It will help your child develop skill and maturity to take decision and handle any situation.

- If your child is yet to get into a primary school and likes to wear such clothes which do not suites to him/her, do not stop him/her from doing so. If your child wears that dress at his/her own wish, he/she will have confidence in it. And thus, he/she will develop the ability to turn his/her shyness into boldness.

✓ Sometimes try to bring some issue (not of much serious nature) to your child and seek his opinion in regard of taking decision or try to know his idea in finding the solution of that problem.
✓ If you find your child's opinion worthwhile, implement it. And if you do not find it workable then also appreciate it telling that he may think and find out better solution also. It will encourage him to apply his intellect more than earlier and thus, he will never let himself down.

Behaviours with Etiquette

As said in previous chapters, your actions work constructively to make your child a gentleman with appreciable social etiquette besides making him a man of strong moral character.

One thing always needs to bear in mind that children replicate and imitate all those actions what their parents or elders in the family do. It mostly involves the parents' mannerism and etiquette as to how they behave and interact with others.

What Can Parents Do?

- Though most of the parents know well how to greet others and shake hands with them, they are advised to do all these good-mannered actions in front of their child.

- Keep eye contact while talking to guests or anyone you meet.

- Using such words of etiquette as "Please," "Thanks," "Excuse me," and "I am sorry" will always brings honour to your child.

- While opening the door for someone, always welcome them warmly with a smile.

- Whenever you are along with your child in any party or feast, first try to offer seat to your elders and ladies, and then think for yourself. You also do this courtesy while travelling in bus, train or elsewhere. It will leave a superb impression upon your child and he/she will understand the value of good mannerism.

- Besides teaching your child social etiquette with your action, you can also teach him/her verbally how to sit, how to behave, how to eat and how to leave the seat on dining table and what should be said while leaving the seat.

- Take your child to excursion, to your relatives and friends and other offices and place of social gathering. Whenever you go somewhere you may carry some luggage with you. If there is less room in the bus or train, just teach your child how to adjust your luggage in the bus/ train without causing inconvenience to co-passengers. At the same time, just have a watch whether there is someone who deserves seat more than you due to being physically challenged or old. If so, take initiative in offering seat to such persons.

- If your child wants to write/say something to someone who might have done something good to him or might have helped him in any manner, just encourage your child to mention the words of thanks and gratitude for them. Younger kids may also send some drawing made by them that contains respect and love latent in the drawings. Though today children know how brief they are in expressing something, you may also guide him to write the words of thanks and gratitude crisply using catchy words.

- While in service or business, you get the chance to write some note of thanks to your seniors and colleagues. While doing so, just show it to your child and tell him how to start writing and how to express the desired things in an impressive way.

- ✓ Neha, you know what a nice thing I've learned today from my Dad?
- ✓ Glad to know it Ruhi, now tell me what you've learned.
- ✓ My dad was arguing with my mom as he was angry at something wrong done by her. Meanwhile we heard the sound of our doorbell. When my dad opened the door, he found his friend standing there. He welcomed him so warmly with a smile, I couldn't believe if it was the same man who was so angry just a few seconds back!!!
- ✓ Yes, this is one of the best examples of social etiquette, patience and mannerism. Your father is a great source of learning. So keep following him and obeying him.

Is Your Home Haunted by Ghost?

Having fear for anything is a natural thing, but sometimes children develop a fear of ghost in their home or around them. This is called hallucination. Children complain of ghost's presence especially in nights and at the places of complete darkness. It seems silly and totally unreasonable.

What Can Parents Do?

- If your child complains of having seen any ghost type entity or heard any scary sound, do not ignore him simply. Just ask what type of shape that entity had; where he saw that terrible ghost; and what type of sound he heard. Whether the shape of that ghost was the same as he had seen in so and so film or TV serials; whether the sound he had heard resemble to the sound which he had heard in so and so horror movie. Sometimes, children fall victim to fear of such things after watching some horror movie or something in TV and even after hearing some stories of adventures and horrors.

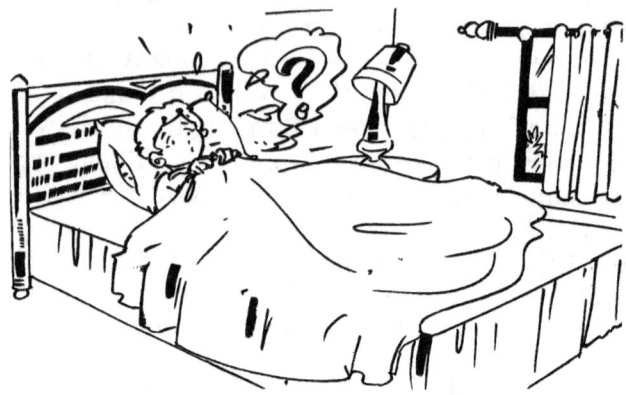

- Sometimes blow of strong wind also makes scary sound which children think the voice created by ghosts. So what you need to do is, take your child outside the house, or take him to the terrace and let hear that sound of the wind. Ultimately, your child will understand well that it was nothing but the sound of the wind that he was scared of.

- Similarly, if your child complains of noticing any shadow or ghost-like entity, keep torch with you. Simply focus that light on the place where your child complains to have seen any scary figure. When he will find nothing of the imagined figure at the focused place, he will realise that it was just his imagination and whim that evolved fear in him.

- As precautionary measures, do not allow your child to watch horror movies, indecent action films or programmes, or play violent video games. According to a research, the fear children experience is the result of watching a horror movie that may last for years also. It affects the children's sleep and other behaviours also. Even your children happen to watch such movies, just convince them telling that all these scary entities and actions they see in the movies are based on imagination and artificiality; they do not have any concern with real life we live.

• Teen-aged children fear the judgements of their peers. They want independence in every sphere of life. So help your child develop a sense of independence from the thoughts of their peers and also from those promoted by media. Encourage your child to adopt his/her own style and ideas that will ultimately work for him/her in a beneficial way.

✓ Children are advised not to fear unnecessarily from imaginary entities or things because such things do not have their existence in reality.
✓ Nights, darkness and isolation (loneliness) do cause fear, but cannot cause any harm to you. So you need not get scary of such environment if you are caught with. Of course, you may take precautions at such places where firing, snatching and robberies are a common phenomenon.
✓ Parents are advised to instill the essence of courage in their children so that they should not be afraid of scary things.

Realisation and Apology

It doesn't mean that only children can commit mistakes and go out of the right track; adults, and even parents also do a lot of mistakes and often swerve from the righteous path. So if you, as parents, commit any wrong thing before your child, be honest to confess it and say sorry for having done so.

What Can Parents Do?

- If any of your acts sets a bad example of treatment, try to be honest before your child in accepting the wrong you have done. It will not only let your child learn the virtue of realisation and apology but also enhance your honour in his eyes.

- If your behaviour has been watched by your child and he appears to be fault-finding for you, try to be honest to him telling 'yes' you have done this and you are apologetic for the same with an assurance that such thing will not be repeated in future.

- If you happen to treat someone badly—maybe it could have been due to something wrong done by others; even then also, approach him and say sorry for doing so. This noble act will enhance your honour in the eyes of that person whom you have mistreated as well as in the eyes of your child.

✓ Your courage and honesty exuded in accepting the fault/wrong done by you and your realisation with the words of apology and sorry will help your child strengthen his/her moral character besides letting him/her learn the will to take stand at any moment of such situation.

Take Stand for Your Self-respect

Being polite and courteous is a basic essence of good moral character, but it doesn't mean to keep tolerating the cruelties consistently meted out to you by someone, who takes it as your weakness. So stand up for yourself and be strict to force others to confess their fault and apologise for their offence if they do anything wrong to you.

What Can Parents Do?

- If your child is of play school level or under the age of 3-4 years, play with him in an open place like park or garden etc. You may leave him liberally to play at his own wish or let him sit at any particular place. And then keep watching what others in the park do with him. Of course, most of the people would love him and try to play with him. But there may be a few who may not do so. They may try to snatch ball from him or try to scare him. At that time, take stand and elicit from him the reason behind doing so. This will increase your trust in you and thus, he will attain courage also.

- When you happen to confront with some odd situation, you must stand up for yourself and let your child see that though you do it with strictness and firmness, yet without losing the virtue of courtesy and good judgement.

- When you go to buy something in the market along with your child, and the shopkeeper charges much more than the reasonable price. At that time you bargain with the shopkeeper to charge the reasonable price. At that time, you may test your child's I.Q. asking him what should be done. What he says in this regard. If your child tells you to leave and go for another shop, ask him the reason. And if he tells you buy in the same price as put by the shopkeeper then also ask him why he should do so.

- Teasing is a common pastime by naughty boys. So help your child learn how to deal with when someone teases him. It's a matter of necessary concern because children who get upset easily by teasing may become weak and fall an easy victim to bullies. When you've listened thoroughly to your child's story of being teased, help him find a "bully-protecting strategy" with which he finds himself protected. Just keep in mind that what works for your child may not work for others; and what works for one situation is not necessary that it will also work in another situation. Some strategies that your child may find effective may be the following:

- Ask the teaser why he would tell so.

- Show your strictness, firmness and courage by telling the teaser, "I want you to stop teasing me; otherwise be ready to face tough time."

- Teaser may ridicule you on hearing such words of firmness and courage. But you may tell him, "I think you are deaf and dumb, but I am not."

- If the teaser again makes the mockery of your words, you may respond him with a simple word of "So?" or "Thanks for saying so."

- There is also an effective way of warding off the teasing and that is, just ignore the teasing. Do not bother about it, and simply walk away from there without looking at the teaser as if he doesn't have any value in front of you.

- These strategies will help your child overcome the oddities of teasing. So advise your child to keep calm, maintain composure, speak firmly and look the teaser in the eye without resorting to teasing him back to revenge the insult.

- The best way to remedy this evil thing is to report this matter to an elder, teacher, parents so that they can stand up for your help and rebuke or take any punitive action against the teaser or make the teaser realise what wrong he has been doing and what could be its consequences.

- If the situation takes a serious turn and the teasing goes even to the perils of your child's life, you must swing into action by intervening into the case. Take up this case to proper authorities which can solve the problem.

✓ It is incumbent upon the children to learn the appropriate ways of dealing with the unpleasant behavior of others. Others may create obstacles and problems in your ways by adopting any evil measure. But you need not bother about it. Face it boldly by ignoring it and bothering least about it.

Help Yourself

With the growing of age, children will continue to get newer responsibilities where they are to make their contributions accordingly.

What Can Parents Do?

• With the passage of time, your child moves towards the age of maturity. So as parents, you may decide what kinds of responsibilities your child can take up and accomplish satisfactorily. Start giving him responsibilities to accomplish and simultaneously keep teaching him how to do them. With his success in accomplishment, gradually increase the impetus of responsibilities that will strengthen your child physically and mentally.

- While giving the responsibilities and teaching your child how to accomplish them, you must tell them that he can do it well and he has the ability to do it well and that's why you are expecting from him so.

- If your child is younger, you get some work done by him showing him and getting it done as fun. Gradually, he will take the completion of such chores as fun and attain expertise in tackling such tasks.

- In course of time, you may give some tasks to your child and before that just ask him how he will do it. If you are not satisfied with his way he unravels, teach him how to do it.

- When you are ironing your clothes, polishing your shoes and packing your luggage while moving on tour; display these demos to your child so that he may also try and become self-dependent. Learning of such chores will help him throughout his life.

- Besides showing the demos of daily chores that you try to teach your child, it is also necessary that you teach him the importance of learning and doing so. There are places where you will not find any laundry to press your clothes and polish boys to polish your shoes. If you join defence forces like Army, Navy and Air Force etc., the cadets are supposed to do all these daily chores themselves. Even if you happen to live in a hostel of school, college or university, most of the borders of these hostels do their daily chores themselves. So one must be prepared to overcome such difficulties of life.

✓ Learning to do daily chores help the children accomplish bigger responsibilities in life. So initially, they must take them as fun so that they should not get bored while doing them. Moreover, if children learn doing chores and thus accomplishing responsibilities, they become self-dependent and will be able to teach their children in future.

When Chores Become Bigger Responsibilities

In the initial phase of teaching your ways and importance of doing chores and accomplishing responsibilities, explain to him that doing daily chores is just one kind of responsibility. Gradually, it will grow in quantity, quality, and impetus, even in risks as well. If he becomes responsible to do the tasks assigned to him, it means he is answering for actions and words, becoming dependable and trustworthy and making use of perfect judgement. So let your child realise that exuding these qualities is a good indication that will make him a person of trust and responsibility to be appreciated by all.

What Can Parents Do?

- Watch such movie or a TV show with your child in which you can find the characters playing the roles that involve responsibilities. After watching the movie/TV show, just asked your child which character he found more responsible and dutiful. Put second question to clarify if that character had not did justice to his responsibilities what would have been the consequence. Add another question asking him whether the character would have gone for another option also. If you find your child's answers appropriate and satisfactory, appreciable; and if not, explain him what would be the correct answers to these questions.

- Be attentive to know what your child's opinion is on the decisions that involve committing the right thing. Appreciate him for his opinion and if you find it irrelevant then explain him what is correct and what is wrong.

- If your child acts responsibly and answer your questions satisfactorily, appreciate your him/her by saying such encouraging words as "Well done," "I am proud of you," "You will glorify the name of our family and nation" and so on.

✓ It's been noticed that some parents reward their children with precious gifts, money and allowing more time to watch movies/TV shows etc. for acting responsibly. But this is not a better idea. They should be taught to convince that their acts done with responsibility are itself a reward for them.

Heroic Deeds

When the word 'hero' is delivered or read, an image of film (reel) hero automatically comes to our mind. It's also a source of inspiration and encouragement to our children to learn something constructively. So the parents are advised to share with their children the heroic tales of real heroic actors. You may also tell your children to open history books and learn how the kings and their soldiers mustered their courage and never yielded themselves while fighting the battles.

Better to Have

Children are advised to have photographs of real heroes in their drawing rooms and album as their pictures will keep inspiring them to do heroic acts that always bring benefits to family, society and nation. etc.

What Can Parents Do?

- Discuss with your child on real hero and their heroic deeds. Ask him what acts and accomplishments make them able to be called "heroes" in real life.

- Due to having a generation gap and being much older than your children, you have heard and gone through much stories of valour and even seen many of such brave persons. You may have also seen some men of heroic deeds in your family or in your location. So when you sit together with your child, tell the stories of such brave persons that will enhance your child's courage and inspiration to do something great in life.

- There may have also been some widows who have shown their courage and calibre to sustain their children in absence of their husbands and might have overcome several terrible adversities and difficulties in sustaining their children. It's also a great act of bravery and wisdom, which women show after being widowed. So you may also refer their stories of struggle and courage to your child to instil in him the courage to face the challenges of life in future.

- In your location/society, here may have been also such children who after being orphaned and having no help from others, had to struggle hard for their survival. Resultantly, they not only survived but also made great successes in life. You can also tell such didactic real stories to your children to make them strong enough to face successfully such challenges in life.

✓ Stories, especially the real ones of hard struggles, adventures and subsequent successes instill the elements of courage and inspiration among children. So the children must focus on how the characters of the stories turn their poverty into prosperity and how they turn their failure into success.

How Can I Be of Help to Someone?

It's so easy to be of help to someone. To become charitable doesn't mean to give alms (money) to needy people only. You may also become charitable by helping someone serve medicine, sacrificing your seat in bus or train for any more deserving person than you, assisting someone sit on wheelchair and even removing aside banana peel from the main road lest anybody should fall down by slipping from it, and so on.

What Can Parents Do?

- Parents are urged to act charitably before their child as their charitable or philanthropic acts will be a great lesson and source of guidance to your child.

- Often talk with your child about the importance of extending help to those who are need. Teach him that such services which are in fact philanthropic in nature make child a perfect citizen with great deeds and feats that add honour to his personality.

- Teach your child that children can serve the society and humanity in accordance with their age, maturity and physical and mental growth. A little kid can help a beggar by giving him a few coins from his piggy bank. But grown up children can also accomplish the task of collecting fund to rehabilitate the victims of any natural calamity in the country besides doing other charitable works where huge and collective, physical and financial power is required.

- You can show the works of volunteers (some of them maybe of celebrity status as Bollywood actor Vivek Oberoi had voluntarily reached Cuddalur in Tamil Nadu to serve the tsunami victims) through news reports when they join the bandwagon of philanthropists to serve the humanity in the time of emergency and crises.

✓ According to a research, the children participating in community and humanity service programmes, especially when these concern with teamwork to rehabilitate the victims of natural calamities, are found becoming the persons of great contributions to their character-building.

Cope with Courage

Hardships in human life are a common phenomenon. But one should not lose one's courage to cope with the hardships that come in different forms. Besides courage, children need to learn the skills and qualities that will help them get rid of difficulties and make life peaceful and pleasant.

What Can Parents Do?

- Resilience is the main essence of bravery. Tell your child if two wrestlers—one much stronger, while his rival shorter and weaker in comparison, start fighting in a wrestling ring. The weaker one is put to the ground repeatedly by the stronger one but all the times the physically weaker wrestler stands up and challenges the stronger wrestler to resume the fight. This is called resilience. Thus, by giving such example you can talk with your child about resilience one must have in facing any type of hardship and difficulty in life. The hardships may be of different forms like losing money or health, or being bereaved of the beloved ones owing to death or break-ups in relations.

• Convince your child to take it granted that resilient people are blessed with the asset of resilience that never let them frustrate in any form. According to researchers, those who do not lose resilience have certain qualities as given below:

Qualities of Being Resilient

- Able to make strategies and implement them
- Always sustain positive view about oneself
- Be confident of one's abilities
- Having firm belief in one's strengths
- Possessing superb communication skill
- Able to solve problems
- Able to maintain composure in panicky situations
- Able to manage any sudden or persistent urge

Qualities of Being Social

- Being caring for others and careful about oneself
- Must know as to who loves him
- Must have a role model who could be a celebrity or a common man
- Better to have an elder from one's family, locality, or nation whom he can interact and accept as his role model

✓ A child can strengthen his relations with an adult/elder from his family, society or even nation whom he can consider his role model for his qualities. The child must assure in his role model the quality of being resilient and bolstering others to have resilience besides other requisite qualities.

Choice of Good Friends

There is no dearth of friends, but what matters the most is whether they have the qualities of being your friends. There are several boys and girls who can respond you positively on offering friendship but very few of them deserve to be your friend with requisite traits of friendship. So children need to be very choosy in making friends and always use their wisdom while proceeding for that.

What Can Parents Do?

- Sit together with your child and just ask what according to him a friend is and how a good friend ought to be.

- Teach your child the skill to tell his friend that he will not continue his friendship with someone whom he has befriended, in a way that his friend should not take his statement in a wrong way.

- Parents must know who their child's friends are and how they are by nature and character. To assess their qualities, invite them to your home or take them on an excursion to a park or bowling alley. While interacting and playing with them, observe their behaviour and listen to what they think and say to each other. You need to do this to know with whom your child spends his time. Sometimes your child chooses some friends who are not good by nature or character. Such friend circle may sway your child away from the righteous track making him a boy of faulty character. So you need to be cautious in this regard.

✓ Childhood, especially in adolescence, is found to be an unstable phase of life. So it is incumbent upon the children to be cautious in making friends. They must take guidance from their parents, teachers and family elders in choosing friends and assessing their nature and character before befriending them.

Respond to Your Feelings

When children or even adults watch anything or adopt it, they have certain feelings about it. This feeling should not go unattended. So children should respond to their feelings and take decisions accordingly in having felt about someone good or bad and raising question to themselves why they felt like that. It will help them distinguish the typed of people they meet and interact.

What Can Parents Do?

- Teach your child how to identify his feelings. Talk with him categorically about how you feel about a particular thing and how he feels about it.

- Whenever you tell a story to your child or watch a movie/TV show along with him, discuss with him about his feelings for different characters that played different roles.

- Convince your child that sometimes the way people think about certain things affects the way they feel. If your child is bothered about something, help him test his thoughts and make change in those thoughts so that he may feel better. For example, your child in teens may be anxious as to how he will secure a job and will be able to support himself as well as his family. At such juncture, you simply advise him to concentrate on his studies and other concrete things rather than bothering much about his job and livelihood.

✓ More often, our feelings caution us about good and bad things besides cautioning us what we should do in which situation and who should be trusted. Thus, feelings play an important in distinguishing many things in life.

Sharing Your Experiences

Whether it is a story you have read or heard or any astonishing thing you have experienced, better you share all these things with your child. By listening to you and coming to know about such things, your child will be able distinguish the good and bad qualities of the characters and thus, gradually he himself will be able to decide right things about him. Of course, with the advent of Internet and YouTube children have developed their interest in watching movies and shows rather than listening to or reading stories, yet reading stories aloud by themselves will be more effective and constructive in their character-building.

What Can Parents Do?

- Collect good books of didactic stories. Slash time from your busy schedule and devote it to reading the stories from these books aloud and let your children read them aloud. After the book is read, try to know from your children what they have understood about the behaviours of the characters in the stories. Put another question asking him whether any of character resemble to those of their own life. Subsequently, encourage especially your teen-aged children to find such books and read the stories from them that will help them understand the different characters and qualities of people living around them.

- After the stories are read, ask your children which character they like the most and why. You may also ask why that character they consider to be important in human life. You may further ask what were the motives of behaving well and doing good by the characters they liked and what were the motives of the negative characters who do bad for others? In other words, you may also ask as thus: Which characteristics make that particular character the hero of the story and which traits make that particular character the villain of the story?

- Different family members have different tastes of reading materials as some of them may go for reading poems, articles and editorials etc. But your duty as parents should be to set aside time for the family to get the stories read aloud by them, making this act more interesting and beneficial.

- Make sure your home does not lack in good reading materials and also ensure that it's not necessary that reading materials should not be new and expensive. You can find such materials at city's weekly book hat, ordinary bookstalls, and in library sales. At the same time, encourage the members in your friend circle, relatives and acquaintances giving gifts of books on special occasions to children instead of toys, jewelleries, gadgets, etc.

- Persuade your child to visit library for books. Take him/her to local library and help him/her obtain his/her own library card. To meet the purpose, you may request the librarian to help your child locate different racks in the library and use the library catalogue to find the interesting materials.

- Whenever you pay a visit to the library along with your child, you also check out some books for yourself. Your exuding interest in collecting books and reading them will make you a role model of reading for your child. Thus, let your child watch you reading and benefiting from it.

- Of course, watching something important on TV or YouTube is also a source of benefit for children, but excess of this lead to nowhere except confusion and addiction. Something read with interest is hardly forgotten in future as one can recall those didactic things in a jiffy faster than clicking mouse on computer.

✓ Simply reading and forget all about it will not work for children. Subsequent to reading a story, there is a need to start a question-answer session in which parents should ask the children regarding the characters played in the play/story and relate the positive ones to their lives.

✗ ✗ ✗

How To Cope with Media Pressure

"Children are our second chance to have a great parent-child relationship."
~ *Laura Schlessinger*

Undoubtedly, today media is so influencing and aggressive that it can sway people to any direction, pressurising them to accept what it brings to them. Those in media business are increasing their TRP (Television Rating Point) and thus, earning huge money. Moreover, media has evolved into such a power of attraction that it can also play a leading role in moulding our character into a shape that it wants. When we spot the word 'Media' it means shows, programmes and advertisements made available by Internet, TV, radio, newspapers, movies, and all that we get from these resources. However, Internet and TV are leading among them. In other words, we all, including our children, have come under media pressure and have become slave to media only because of its glamour.

Undoubtedly, media has helped our children increase their knowledge of different fields, but their greed to earn more in stiff competition has made many TV channels and print journals to show any rubbish—violence and vulgarity, losing the decency which they had in the beginning.

Here are some effective tips that will help your child escape and get rid of media pressure:

- Sit together with your child and discuss on the media pressure upon people, especially the children. Try to teach your child that it is media that just for their TRP and earning, entice the viewers to adopt and accept what media is showing to them. Thus, more often people are misled by the media. So there is need to not get influenced by the media false and momentary glitters.

- Media pressurises us to accept their appeals in various ways. So there is need to help your child identify the various kinds of pressure he faces daily from TV, newspapers, journals, billboards, music, glamorous shows, movies, video games and so on.

- Make your child aware of the consequences of adopting and rejecting the messages brought by media to him. These may consist of how to make your body muscular like so and so star, how you can mark your presence by putting these designer clothes and so on. Such things need to be tackle with wisdom and self-control.

Let Your Child Adopt the Two-optioned Refusal Method

- After checking out the message, apply the 'self-respect process': Confirm whether it makes you feel awkward about yourself. Whether you find people treating each other as you wish to be treated.

- If the answer is positive, waste no time to abstain from being impressed by doing any of those given below:

  - Just change the channel/station, go to another page, stop the game you are playing.

  - Put the TV off, do the same with song, game, or radio, or put aside the journal you are reading or get away from the place where the message is being presented.

- Resume your talk to the message with a positive counter-message.

- Ridicule the message.

✖ ✖ ✖

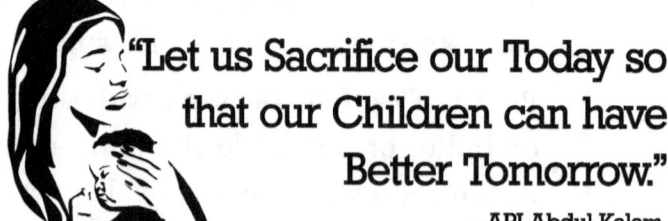

"Let us Sacrifice our Today so that our Children can have Better Tomorrow."

-APJ Abdul Kalam

Visit Schools and Consult Teachers for Character-Building

"The true character of a society is revealed in how it treats its children."
~ *Nelson Mandela*

According to a research, children take the values seriously only if they find their respectable adults give acceptance to adoption of those values. Of course, parents ought to be the source of determining which values their children want to develop, yet they must seek the help of the community, especially the schools of their children to enhance those values. Some effective suggestions are given here regarding what and how the parents should interact with their children's teachers and work with by visiting their schools and meeting other officials of the schools to ensure whether they all hold the unanimous opinion in terms of the basic values that parents want in their children to instil:

- Pay visit to your child's school early in the school year, meet his/her teachers and seek their suggestion in regard of enhancing values in your child. Express yourself as to what type of personality you want to see in your child. Exchange your views with the teachers asking them how they and the school can reinforce the lessons they are teaching your child in character-building.

- If the school is facilitated with a character education programme, or if character education is there in the curriculum, seek the details of the programme or curriculum from the school authorities and discuss with teachers on how you can help reinforce the lessons making it as homework. If a character education programme is not there in the school, involve yourself in the work with the school and local community to start a programme of such kind.

- Share your views with other parents and work with them in groups to help your child's school to initiate and maintain an appreciable standard for behaviour both in school and in the events beyond the school that may include sports events or concerts etc. Help to make a list of volunteers to oversee and organise school activities or educational tours to museums, libraries and places of other edutainment activities. Moreover, you can also interact with other parents to know whether they also agree on standards of behaviour for activities performed beyond the school premises like parties, picnic and educational tours.

✗✗✗

Discover Simple, Super Effective ways to Make your Child A Reader

DON'T ONLY DREAM, MAKE IT TRUE.

We give wings to your
DREAMS

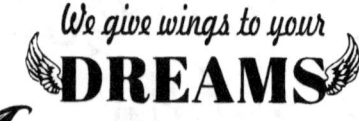

PUBLISH BOOK AND BECOME AN AUTHOR

We will help you to write and share it with world

Visit: Gullybaba.com

www.ingramcontent.com/pod-product-compliance
Lightning Source LLC
Chambersburg PA
CBHW072016170626
46813CB00005B/2162